P9-DWK-815

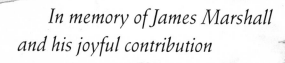

*In memory of James Marshall
and his joyful contribution*

Copyright ©1994 by Bobette McCarthy

All rights reserved.

First edition 1994

Library of Congress Cataloging-in-Publication Data
McCarthy, Bobette.
Dreaming / Bobette McCarthy.—1st ed.
Summary: Asleep in his cozy bed, a dog dreams of
a midnight row out to sea.
ISBN 1-56402-184-X
[1. Dogs—Fiction. 2. Dreams—Fiction. 3. Sleep—Fiction.
4. Stories in rhyme.] I. Title.
PZ7.M478412Dr 1994 [E]—dc20 93-2882

10 9 8 7 6 5 4 3 2 1

Printed in Hong Kong
The pictures in this book were done in watercolor and pen and ink.

Candlewick Press
2067 Massachusetts Avenue
Cambridge, Massachusetts 02140

Dreaming

by Bobette McCarthy

CANDLEWICK PRESS

CAMBRIDGE, MASSACHUSETTS

Drifting and dreaming,

I'm called from my sleep

At high tide,
By moonlight,
Out on the deep.

Where am I going?
What will I see?

The moon knows my name
And is calling to me.

Awash and away,
I drift through the night,

Through mizzle and moonmist,
Through darkness, through light.

Drifting and listing,
I come to the end,

From daytime, through nighttime,

To daytime again.